Alexander Pushkin

THE GOLDEN COCKEREL

and other stories

РИСУНКИ ЯНА ЛЕБИЩА • БРАТИСЛАВА • 1962

THE GOLDEN COCKEREL
and other stories by

ALEXANDER PUSHKIN

English version by
JAMES REEVES
pictures by JÁN LEBIŠ

FRANKLIN WATTS, INC.
575 LEXINGTON AVENUE,
NEW YORK 10022, U.S.A.

First published in Great Britain and the United States, 1969

Co-production with Mladé Letá, Bratislava
Printed in Czechoslovakia

Library of Congress Catalog Card No. 68-16016

PUSHKIN AND THE FIVE FAIRY TALES

ALEXANDER PUSHKIN was the most brilliant and original Russian of his period. Turbulent, outspoken, he both charmed and shocked the Court, where he was constantly the focus of intrigue. And, to him, poetry, like life itself, was not to be confined to accepted topics; his imagination ranged over the whole of experience.

At a time when only foreign art was admitted in Russia (Italian ballet and opera, the works of Byron, Schiller and Goethe or the French philosophers), and when writers still depended on the approval and patronage of the Court, Pushkin had the temerity to seek inspiration from his own country's tradition—and from the peasants, at that!

Storytelling was a very specific part of the Russian heritage which had been transmitted for centuries from generation to generation. Pushkin collected much material, not all of which has survived. In 1824, confined to his country estate by order of the Tsar, the poet wrote down seven folk tales from the mouth of his old nurse, Arina Rodionovna Matveyeva. On three of these he later based *The Tale of Tsar Saltan*, *The Tale of the Parson* and *The Tale of the Dead Princess*. The Grimm brothers' collection was the source for *The Tale of the Fisherman*; Washington Irving's *Tales of the Alhambra* (of which Pushkin possessed a French translation) was the source for *The Golden Cockerel*. Pushkin wrote in the formal six iambic feet of the Alexandrine line, bending the folk material to his own poetic purpose.

The tales thus retold are little gems: it was a revelation to all to see such fine work spring from what had been regarded as a crude, unliterary source. But it was typical of Pushkin's fertile genius that he should see the ingredients of poetry everywhere. His achievement in transmuting into beautiful poems these simple stories had a great influence on other Russian writers.

The present version fulfils a long-felt need. Most of these tales first became known to scholars here through verse translations published in the nineteen-thirties, but for too many years they have been out of print or have not been available in English at all. James Reeves's sensitive prose reproduces Pushkin's stories with fidelity; spare and simple yet full of colour, the language has overtones of meaning for all ages of reader. Not only scholars, but the general reading public, can now enjoy these small masterpieces by Russia's greatest writer.

THE PUBLISHERS

CONTENTS

THE GOLDEN COCKEREL

In a distant kingdom, farther than far, reigned good King Dodon. In youth he had been warlike, never leaving the nearby countries in peace. Time passed. The King grew old. His thoughts turned to peace. To enjoy a life of ease and quiet—that was all he wished for now. But the men of nearby lands wanted revenge. They raided King Dodon's borders, leaving death and destruction behind them. Dodon was forced to keep a large army to do battle all along his frontiers. His soldiers were keen and watchful, but they were never in time to stop the raiders. When Dodon's soldiers marched south, the raiders would turn up in the east. When the soldiers set forth to fight them, they would appear from the sea.

So poor King Dodon wept tears of rage and could not sleep at night.

"I will speak to a wise man," he said, "a magician who understands the stars."

So a rider was sent forth to fetch the magician to the palace. The magician came carrying a bag, and out of the bag he took a golden cockerel.

"O King," he said, "take this bird and set him up on a high steeple. He will be your sentinel. When things are quiet he will sit still. But when there is war or rumour of war he will lift up his red comb, ruffle his bright plumes, crow with all his might and turn towards the threatened danger."

The King was delighted. He thanked the wise man and said:

"For such service no reward is too great. Ask me what you will. Your very first wish shall be granted, even as if it were my own."

So, sitting high up on a steeple, the little cockerel became guardian of Dodon's kingdom. As soon as there was trouble on the borders he would ruffle his feathers, turn towards the danger and sing out:

"Hear my cock-a-doodle shrill!
Sleep in peace and fear no ill."

Then the people on Dodon's borders stopped raiding his kingdom and settled down in peace.

So a year passed and then another. All was peace, and the cockerel was silent on his high perch.

Then one day King Dodon was roused from his slumber by a terrible noise outside his window.

"Wake up, O King and Father of our people!" cried the captain of the guard. "There is bad news."

Dodon sat up and yawned.

"What's all the fuss?" he cried. "What is this dreadful news?"

"The cockerel is crowing fit to burst!" said the captain. "In the city there is panic."

The King looked out of the window. There, sure enough, high on his perch the cockerel was turning to the east, his comb upright, his feathers ruffled.

There was no time to lose. Dodon sent an army eastward under the command of his elder son. At once the cockerel was still. The noise in the city died down. The King went back to bed.

A whole week passed, and no news came from his army. Dodon did not even know if there had been a battle. Then once more the cockerel crowed.

Immediately a second army was sent eastward under the command of the King's younger son, to bring help to his older brother. Again the cockerel was quiet, and again no rider came to the city bringing news.

When another week had passed the same panic seized the people, as once more the cockerel sounded the alarm.

This time the old King decided to lead an army himself, though he was not sure it was wise for him to go.

With Dodon at their head the soldiers marched day and night, mile after mile. They were almost dead

ЦАР

with weariness when, on the eighth day, they came to a range of mountains. On the march to the mountains they were surprised to see neither battle-field nor burial ground. But what they saw at last, in one of the valleys between the mountains, surprised them still more.

A beautiful silken tent fluttered in the breeze, and around it lay the bodies of the King's soldiers, slain in battle. There was utter silence. Dodon hurried to the tent, and there, outside its entrance, he saw the dead bodies of his two sons. Neither had helmet or armour, but each held a sword, thrust into the other's heart. Heads bent, the riderless horses strayed over the blood-soaked grass.

In grief and anguish the King cried out:

"Alas, my sons, and woe betide us all. Who has trapped in his cunning nets our brave falcons?"

And the voices of Dodon's soldiers echoed his words along the desolate valley.

Then the curtains that veiled the entrance to the silken tent were drawn aside. There appeared before the King's eyes the lovely Queen of Shemakhan. Dodon fell silent. As he gazed into the eyes of the Queen, the death of his two sons was forgotten. The Queen smiled at Dodon, curtsied low and took him by the hand. She led him inside her tent. She made him sit at her table and eat of the choicest foods.

When he had finished she let him rest upon her brocaded couch.

For a whole week King Dodon obeyed the Queen's wishes like a slave and passed his time pleasantly in her silken tent.

Then he began to think of returning to his city. His soldiers wanted to go back to their wives. So, taking the fair Queen by the hand, Dodon set out on the journey home.

The news of Dodon's return had gone before him. As he approached the city the crowds came out to welcome him and his young Queen. Dodon graciously thanked the people for their welcome. Then, amidst the crowd, he beheld his old counsellor, the magician. He looked shabby but still wore his magician's hat.

"Greetings to you, wise old man," cried Dodon. "Come closer and tell me how things go with you."

"Greetings, O King," said the magician. "Now is the time for our reckoning. Do you recall how, when I served you in the hour of your need, you promised me anything I might wish? Give me as my reward the beauteous Queen of Shemakhan."

King Dodon was dumbfounded.

"Are you mad?" he demanded. "The devil take you for a madman! True, I promised you all you wished, but you can wish too much. Do you not know who I am? You shall have gold and silver. You shall have a high-sounding title. You shall have the finest horse in my stable or half my kingdom. Any of these things I will give you gladly."

"I want nothing", answered the magician, "but the Queen of Shemakhan."

In a rage Dodon spat on the ground.

"You are too bold, wretched old man," he cried. "You will get nothing—nothing, I say! You had better go while your body is still whole. Take the old fool out of my sight!"

The magician opened his mouth in protest. But Dodon, infuriated, raised his sceptre and struck him on the head. The magician fell dead at the King's feet.

Horror came over the city, and a shudder ran through the crowd. In the terrible silence that followed the shrill laughter of the Queen rang out for all to hear. The King was deeply troubled, but smiled lovingly upon the Queen and told his coachman to drive on. As the royal coach entered the palace gates a rustling sound was heard from above. The golden cockerel flew down from his perch on

the steeple and alighted on the carriage. Then he pecked viciously at the King's head. Dodon toppled from the coach and fell dead on the roadside. The bird flew off into farthest space.

As for the Queen of Shemakhan, she vanished into air and disappeared as if she had never been.

Some say that the ghostly voice of the cockerel was heard to call:

"*This story, be it false or true,*
Something, young men, it may teach you."

THE TALE OF THE FISHERMAN AND THE LITTLE GOLDEN FISH

IN a tumbledown hovel beside the blue, blue sea lived an old fisherman and his wife. They had lived in this same hovel no less than three and thirty years. The old man fished with his nets. The old woman sat spinning.

One day the fisherman cast his net into the water, but, when he drew it in, there was nothing but slime. Next time he cast it, it brought up only seaweed. A third time he cast the net, and this time it held a single fish. It was no ordinary fish. It was of the purest gold, gleaming in the sunlight.

In a voice of terror the little fish cried out for mercy.

"Old man, old man," she cried, "drop me back into the sea and I will give you anything you ask."

The fisherman was surprised and frightened. For

three and thirty years he had been a fisherman, and never before had he heard a fish talk like a human being. He let the golden fish go.

"God be with you, little fish," said he kindly. "I have no need of a reward. Enjoy your freedom in the blue, blue sea.'

He went back home and told his wife about the marvellous thing that had happened.

"Today I caught one little fish. It was a very special one. It was made of gold. She spoke just as we do. She begged me to let her go free. She even offered me a reward—anything I wished. But I daren't take anything from her, so I just let her slip back into the sea."

"Fool!" cried the old woman. "Idiot! Fancy not daring to ask for a reward. You could at least have demanded a new washtub. Look at this cracked old thing!"

The fisherman went back to the blue, blue sea and noticed that it was rather rough. He called to the little golden fish, and at once she appeared out of the waves.

"What do you want, grandfather?" she asked.

The fisherman bowed low and said:

"Forgive me, Highness Fish," he said. "My old woman is very, very cross with me. There is no peace in our house, for she wants a new washtub. Our washtub is all cracked and dented."

"Do not upset yourself," said the little fish. "Go home in peace. You shall have a new washtub."

So the fisherman went back to his wife and saw that she already had a new washtub. But she wasn't pleased. She only scolded him harder than before.

"Fool!" she cried. "Idiot! Fancy asking for a washtub! You could at least have asked for a cottage."

Back went the old man to the blue, blue sea and called to the golden fish once more. Up she swam, asking:

"What do you want, grandfather?"

The fisherman bowed low and said:

"Forgive me, Highness Fish. My old woman is crosser than ever. There is no peace at home, for now she wants a cottage."

"God be with you," said the little fish. "Go home in peace. The cottage is yours."

When the fisherman returned home the tumble-down hovel was gone. In its place stood a neat cottage with a lighted parlour, a whitewashed chimney and strong oak gates. But the old woman sat at the window screaming at her husband at the top of her voice.

"Fool!" she shouted. "Idiot! Fancy asking for a cottage! I don't want to be a poor peasant woman. I want to be a lady of style. Go and bow to your fish again and tell her that!"

The old man returned to the blue, blue sea, and this time the waves looked angry. He called to the golden fish, and she swam up.

"What is it now, grandfather?" she asked.

The fisherman bowed low and said:

"Forgive me, Highness Fish. My old woman is out of her mind. There's no more peace at home. She doesn't want to be a poor peasant woman any more; she wants to be a highborn lady."

"Don't worry," replied the fish. "God be with you."

The old man trudged home to his wife. Instead of the cottage there was a tall castle. At the entrance stood the old woman. She wore a rich fur cloak and a high silk headdress. Round her neck was a great pearl necklace. On her fingers were gold rings, on her feet scarlet boots. She was surrounded by maid-servants. She was pushing them, slapping them, pulling their hair.

"Good day, gracious madam," said the fisherman. "Now at last, perhaps, you have all you desire."

But the old woman only screamed at the old man and sent him off to the stables.

So a week went by, and then another. Then the old woman lost her head once more and sent her husband off to speak to the fish.

"Go and bow to her," she ordered, "and tell her I don't want to be a highborn lady any more. I want to be a queen, do you hear?—a queen!"

The old man shook with fear and said:

"Are you quite mad? You can't walk properly. You can't talk properly. You'll make a fool of yourself before the whole kingdom."

The old woman grew angrier than ever and boxed the old man's ears.

"You lowborn clown!" she said. "Now I am a lady of style. How dare you answer me back? Get back to the sea again, or I'll have you dragged there by force."

The poor old fisherman trudged wearily back to the shore. This time the sea looked black and angry. He called to the little golden fish. She swam up to him and said:

"What is it now, grandfather?"

"Forgive me, Highness Fish," said the old man, bowing low. "My wife is once more in a tantrum. She doesn't want to be a lady of style. She wants to be high and mighty—in fact, she wants to be a queen."

The golden fish replied:

"Don't worry. Go back to your old woman, and God will go with you. Your wife shall have what she wants."

The fisherman went back home, and what did he see but the great halls of a splendid palace! In one of them was sitting his old woman, dressed in the robes of a queen. Boys and noblemen ran to and fro, filling her goblet with the wines of far-off lands. Some brought her dishes of sweet gingerbread. He was almost scared out of his wits. But he made a deep bow before his wife and said:

"Hail, dreaded Empress, high and mighty! Perhaps *now* you have all that your heart can desire."

But the old woman did not so much as glance at him. She only ordered her followers to take him out of her presence. The knights and nobles pushed and jostled him out of the hall. At the great doors the Queen's bodyguard almost cut him in pieces with their axes. As for the common people, they mocked at him and jeered.

"Serves you right, good-for-nothing! When will you learn that a queen's palace is not for the likes of you?"

A week went by, and then another week. Then the old woman almost went out of her mind. She sent her followers to fetch the fisherman. When they found him and dragged him back to the palace, she said:

"Run along, you, and make a bow to your golden fish. I don't want to be just a queen. I want to be ruler of the sea. Then I can live in the blue waves, and your little fish will be my slave and have to do whatever I command."

The old man hadn't the courage to deny her anything. So once more he trudged off to the sea. A great storm was raging, and angry, white-capped waves were foaming all over the ocean. But he called to the little fish, and she swam up to him.

"What is it this time, grandfather?" she asked.

The old man bowed low.

"Oh, forgive me, Highness Fish," he begged. "I simply don't know what to do about my tiresome old woman. She doesn't want to be just a queen any more. She wants to be ruler of the sea and live in it. She wants you to be her slave and do whatever she commands."

The little fish said never a word. With a swirl of her golden tail she disappeared under the sea. For a long time the old fisherman stood by the shore waiting for an answer, but there was no answer. So slowly and sadly he went back to his old woman. To his astonishment the palace had vanished. In its place stood the little old hovel. On the doorstep sat his wife. In front of her was the washtub, cracked and dented as it had been in the beginning.

THE TALE OF THE PARSON AND HIS WORKMAN BALDA

THERE was once a parson who seemed to have very little to do. He used to walk around the market gazing at all the wares. One day he met Balda, who was strolling about in no particular direction.

"What are you looking for?" asked Balda.

"I am looking for a man", answered the parson, "who will serve me as a cook, a stable-boy and a carpenter all in one—and the wages won't be much."

"I'm your man," replied Balda readily. "I'll be your servant. I'll ask no pay except the right to give you three raps on the head at the end of every year."

The parson was surprised and dismayed to hear these terms. But he was a mean man, so he decided to take Balda at his word.

Balda became the parson's man-of-all-work. He toiled from dawn till nightfall. He ate enough for

four, though his food was only porridge. But he worked like seven, attending to the horses, ploughing the soil, lighting the stove, buying and cooking all the food.

The parson's wife was loud in Balda's praises. Their little boy called him "Uncle". The parson alone kept quiet. At the back of his mind all the time was the nagging thought that one day Balda would have to be paid.

"How hard is a rap on the head?" he asked himself.

As the year drew to its close the parson began to lose his sleep and his appetite. At last he decided to tell his wife about it. She was cleverer than he, and at once told him what to do.

"Send Balda on an impossible errand," she said, "something that nobody could do. Tell him that if he can't carry it out he won't get his wages at the end of the year."

"An excellent idea!" said the parson. "That's what I'll do."

He summoned Balda and told him that a certain family of water-devils had promised to pay him ren so long as he lived, but that they hadn't paid him for three years. He ordered Balda to go to the water-devils and collect the rent. Balda took on the job, like any other, and obediently set off for the

lake. He sat on the shore and twiddled the end of a rope in the water. Presently an old devil came to the surface.

"Why are you wrinkling our lake?" he asked.

Balda answered that he would go on wrinkling the lake as long as he liked, and he wished he could make the whole accursed race of devils double up with cramp.

"I have come to collect my master's rent," he said, "which hasn't been paid for three years."

The old devil was worried.

"Stop wrinkling the lake", he said, "and I promise the rent will be paid in full. But first I must see my grandson about it."

At that moment a young devil popped his head out of the water and said that none of them down there had heard anything about rent. However, if Balda would race the imp round the lake the rent would be paid in full to the winner. Balda agreed, but he insisted that not he but his younger brother should race the imp. Then he went into the wood and caught two hares, which he dropped into a sack. When the young imp stood on the shore ready for the race Balda said:

"Here is my young brother. You must race him first. If you beat him, I will take you on myself."

As the young imp darted off Balda let one of the

two hares out of the sack. Instantly it scuttled off into the wood and went back to its form.

When the young imp returned hot and tired, he found Balda holding a hare on his lap. Balda stroked the hare and told him he had done well to run so fast round the lake.

Disappointed, the young imp went back under the water to talk to his grandfather and the other devils. Now Balda wrinkled the water so furiously that there was a storm. The waves divided, exposing the little imp to view. Once more he promised to bring the rent, but said that first they should have a contest as to which could shoot a stick highest into the air. To this Balda answered that he would wait for a cloud so that he could shoot his stick right into it. After that he would have a shot at the devils. The frightened imp once again promised to bring the rent and then went back to his grandfather.

Balda did not wait long. He began to worry the devils with his rope again and make the ocean roar. Again the little devil popped up with his promise to pay over the money. This time it was Balda who said he would set the competition himself.

"Do you see that grey mare over there?" he asked the imp. "If you can lift her and carry her a mile, you can keep the rent. If not, you must pay up every penny."

The little devil crawled under the mare and lay there, heaving and straining. The best he could do was to hoist her up and carry her two paces.

Balda jumped lightly on to the mare's back and shouted:

"How do you think you can do better than me, you miserable little imp? You couldn't lift this

animal between your arms, but I can do it between my legs!"

So saying, he made the mare rear up and prance in the air. Then she galloped a full mile.

So at last all the devils could do was to hand over the money Balda said they owed. A collection was made, and a whole sack was filled with gold pieces. Balda lifted the sack on his shoulder and went back to his master.

When the parson saw him, he was so terrified that he hid behind his wife. But Balda chased him out, handed over the sack of coins and asked for his wages.

At the first rap on the head the parson flew up to the ceiling. At the second rap he completely lost his speech. At the third he lost his wits.

"It serves you right, father," said Balda. "You've tried too hard to get everything for nothing!"

THE TALE OF THE DEAD PRINCESS AND THE SEVEN BRAVE KNIGHTS

THERE was once a King who went on a long journey. He left the good Queen at home, for she was expecting her first child. She missed the King very much and passed her days at the window watching for his return. There was nothing for the Queen to gaze at but a great desert of snow stretching on for ever. Nothing came to end her loneliness.

At last, on Christmas Day, God sent her a baby daughter, and on the selfsame day the King came back. But the joy and excitement of these events were too much for the poor Queen. Before morning mass had been sung in the palace chapel she was dead.

For a whole year the King wept and mourned. But time lessens grief, and even a king cannot bear loneliness for ever. When the year of mourning was over he took a second wife. She was a princess, tall

and stately. Her skin was smooth and white, but her temper was black and ugly. She was vain, jealous, overbearing. She brought with her a magic mirror—a mirror that would talk to her and her alone. She loved to fondle it and ask it questions. She would say to it:

"*Mirror, mirror on the wall,*
Whose is the fairest face of all?"

Then the mirror would tell the new Queen that she herself was the fairest. At this she would look vainer than ever, laugh with delight, clap her hands and perform a little dance.

Meanwhile the little Princess, daughter of the dead Queen, grew and grew. As a bud turns into a flower, she blossomed into a most beautiful maiden. Her brows and lashes were dark, her skin white and fair. The King adored her, and in due time decided she should be married. He found her the handsomest of bridegrooms, the Prince Elisey. As a dowry for his daughter he gave the Prince seven market towns and a hundred and forty great halls.

On the eve of the wedding there was to be a party for the bride. The Queen, as she adorned herself in all her finery, looked into her mirror and asked it her usual question:

"Mirror, mirror on the wall,
Whose is the fairest face of all?"

But this time the mirror answered:

"Fair as thou art in all thy pride,
Fairer and sweeter is the bride."

The Queen was furious.

"You lie!" she screamed, hurling it to the floor and kicking it aside. "You are lying just to torment me."

Then she added spitefully:

"No wonder the Princess is so white and fair. When her mother was expecting her, she had nothing to look at but a waste of snow. But I'm not going to be beaten by this chit of a girl. I shall get rid of her once and for all."

She sent for Chernavka, one of her maids, and told her to take the Princess to the forest, tie her to a tree and leave her there for the wolves. Chernavka dared not disobey the young Queen, but once she was in the forest with the innocent Princess she was overcome by pity. The girl begged the maid to let her go, and Chernavka gave in.

Back in the palace Chernavka told the Queen that she had tied the Princess to a tree, where the wolves would certainly take care of the rest.

But the disappearance of the bride on the eve of her wedding caused alarm and commotion throughout the country. The King, in grief and despair, refused to see anyone. But Prince Elisey, sending up a prayer to heaven, resolved to go in search of his lost bride.

All this time the poor Princess wandered here and there through the forest. At last she came to the gates of a great house. A hound ran out and barked, but, as soon as he saw the Princess, he stopped

barking and began to play around her with the utmost friendliness. The Princess and the hound went through the gates together. In the courtyard all was silent. The dog followed the girl to the porch, fawning upon her and running this way and that. The girl went up the steps and quietly opened the door. Inside was a well-lit parlour. There were seats covered with rugs, there were oak tables and a tiled stove. It had the look of a sitting-room for good, well-behaved people. So, after the girl had looked round the room, she tidied it up and kindled a fire in the stove. Next she lit a candle in front of the holy image. Then she felt tired, so she climbed the stairs to the attic and was soon fast asleep.

Towards dinner time the sound of horses' hooves was heard in the courtyard. Then seven bearded young knights entered the house. They at once noticed how clean and tidy everything looked. The eldest of the knights called out:

"Ho there, whoever you are! Come out and show yourself. If you are old, you shall be our adopted uncle. If you are young, you shall be our brother. If you are an ancient lady, we will honour you as if you were our mother; and if you are young and pretty, we will make you our sister."

Shyly the Princess came down from the attic. She

curtsied low before the young knights, and in a voice full of hesitation told them what had happened to her. As soon as she spoke, however, the knights guessed that she was a princess. They gave her a seat in the inglenook beside the stove and served

her with food and wine. But she ate and drank little, and afterwards went up again to rest.

Time went swiftly in the forest. Each day, long before dawn, the brothers were off on horseback to shoot the grey duck or to sport with each other in mock tourneys against Saracens or Tartars or Circassian bandits from Pyatigorsk. Meanwhile their young guest kept house for them. She swept and cleaned, prepared the meals and left everything neat and tidy. She never had a cross word for any of them.

It was not long before all seven knights were in love with her. So one morning they all went into her room, and the eldest asked her to choose one of them as her husband. Then the Princess burst into tears and said:

"Alas, dear brothers, I am not free. I am betrothed to Prince Elisey, and I must be faithful to him."

In deep disappointment the brothers left her in peace. Life went on as before, calm, friendly and affectionate.

What was happening at the palace all this time? The Queen had got over her rage, so she took out her mirror from under the seat and asked the usual question:

> "*Mirror, mirror on the wall,*
> *Whose is the fairest face of all?*"

Much to the Queen's surprise, the mirror answered:

> "*Though thou art lovely, fairest Queen,*
> *A maiden in the forest green*
> *Fairer and sweeter may be seen.*"

The Queen was furious. She sent for the maid

Chernavka, whom she nagged and wheedled into confessing what she had done.

In the house in the forest the Princess sat spinning beside her window as she waited for the brothers to return. To her surprise she heard the hound growling angrily in the courtyard. Looking down, she saw that an ancient crone dressed in black was trying to get in.

"This must be a nun come to beg for bread," she said to herself.

So she called out:

"Never mind the dog. I'll come and calm him down."

She ran out to give the old woman a loaf of bread. To the Princess's amazement the hound would not be quiet, but went on snarling and would not let the old woman come in. So the Princess threw the loaf to the old woman over the dog's head, and the woman threw her in return a golden apple. The girl caught it neatly in one hand. The ancient crone vanished, but the hound went on snarling and growling as if he were trying to say something to his mistress.

The princess went back to her spinning, but the apple looked so tempting that she could not resist it. She left off spinning and took a bite. No sooner had she swallowed the morsel than she fell to the ground, dead.

Shortly afterwards the seven brothers came back from their morning's sport. To their dismay they were greeted by the hound, whining and whimpering from sheer misery.

"Something is wrong," they said. "This means ill fortune."

As they entered the parlour, they at once saw the Princess stretched out on a bench beneath the holy image. Yapping with fury, the hound snatched up the rest of the golden apple and instantly dropped dead, for it must have been steeped in poison.

In vain the brothers tried to revive the Princess. In deepest sorrow they waited another three days. They could not bring themselves to give up the sister they all loved. Then it was decided not to bury her in the earth, but to lay her in a coffin of purest crystal. This would be placed in a deep cave far off in the mountains. Sadly the seven knights bore the crystal coffin to the cave. There they raised six columns, from which they suspended the coffin by chains. Slowly and sorrowfully they took leave of her, and there she lay as calm, as lovely as if she were asleep.

The Queen, meanwhile, was expecting the return of her maid Chernavka with good news. She took out her mirror and asked it the same question as before. This time the mirror answered simply:

"Thine is the fairest face of all."

In the meantime poor Prince Elisey, sad at heart, strayed about the country in search of his bride. No one could tell him anything of her. At last, in sheer despair, he asked the sun where she was. The sun could not say, but told the Prince to appeal to the moon. The moon could not tell him either, but said he seemed to remember that he had heard the wind murmuring something about the lost Princess. So

the Prince called to the storm wind and begged him to say what he knew. At last the storm wind spoke:

"Beyond the quiet stream rises a lofty mountain. In the middle of it there is a deep cave. In the cave is a crystal coffin suspended by chains. Inside the coffin is your bride."

The wind flew on, and the Prince broke into tears on hearing that his lovely Princess was dead. Nevertheless he resolved to go to find her. He crossed the stream and reached the mountain. There he found the cave and in it the coffin of pure crystal in which the Princess lay. In an agony of despair he fell to the ground. As he fell he struck the coffin so violently

that it came apart. The Princess in all her beauty awoke from sleep and looked about her in astonishment. Then she sank into the Prince's arms. Quickly Elisey carried her out of the cave and turned his steps homeward.

News of the Princess's return travelled fast through the land. In the castle the Queen was sitting before the mirror. How she delighted to hear herself called fairest of all! Then suddenly the mirror changed its tune and said:

"That thou art fair is not denied:
But fairer is the Prince's bride."

These words were like a dagger in the Queen's heart. Furiously she jumped up, flung the mirror down and crushed it to splinters with her heel. Then she ran out into the courtyard at the very moment when the Prince and the Princess entered in triumph.

The shock was too much for the Queen to bear, and she fell down, dead.

Not long after the funeral Elisey and the Princess were married. A splendid wedding ceremony was held, and the bride and bridegroom lived happily ever afterwards.

THE TALE OF
THE TSAR SALTAN
OF HIS SON
THE FAMOUS AND PUISSANT
CHAMPION PRINCE GVIDON
AND OF THE LOVELY
SWAN PRINCESS

THREE sisters sat spinning beside a window in the dusk, talking quietly among themselves.

"If I were Queen," said the first of them, "I would give a feast for everyone in Christendom."

"If I were Queen," said the second, "I would with my own fingers spin enough linen for the whole kingdom."

"If I were Queen," said the third sister, "I would bear my husband a prince who should be a hero."

No sooner had the third sister spoken than the door opened silently, and the Tsar entered the room. He had been standing just outside, listening to the girls' talk. The last words had pleased him the most.

"Greetings to you, maiden," said the Tsar. "You have spoken well. You shall be my Queen and shall bear me a son who shall be a hero. As for you, good

sisters, one of you shall be the royal weaver. The other shall be cook-in-chief."

So they all went to the Tsar's palace, and the wedding was celebrated that very evening. A feast was held for Tsar Saltan and his newly wedded bride, and, after the guests had departed, the royal couple were left together in peace.

In the kitchen the new chief cook stamped with fury, and the new royal weaver shed tears over her loom. As for the bride, she alone was happy, meaning to do her very best to keep her promise to the Tsar.

At that time the country was at war. After the

honeymoon Tsar Saltan leaped on his horse. He bade his wife farewell, begged her never to forget their love and to take care of herself. While he was still valiantly fighting far from home his wife gave birth to a son who was nearly three feet tall. She cared for the baby as a mother bird cares for its young, and she sent a messenger to her husband the Tsar to give him the good news. But her two sisters, the weaver and the cook, helped by Babarikha the old matchmaker, put their heads together and planned how they might deceive her. They stopped the messenger and sent another one in his place. They told him to say to the Tsar that his wife had

given birth to a son—or a daughter: they really couldn't say which, as it was such a strange little creature, more like a mouse or a frog than a human being.

When he heard this news the Tsar was mad with rage and almost had the messenger hanged. But he became calmer and sent him back to the palace with another message.

"Wait for the Tsar's return and he will decide what to do about the baby."

The messenger rode off and in time reached home. The weaver and the cook and old Babarikha the matchmaker stopped the messenger and gave him so much to drink that he became fuddled. Then they searched him, took away his message and put another in its place. This was the order brought by the tipsy messenger:

"The Tsar commands his guard to take the Queen and her infant at once and cast them into the bottomless sea."

There was nothing to be done but to obey this cruel order. The guards grieved a little over the young Queen and her son as they crowded into the royal chamber and broke the terrible news. Then they took a great barrel and covered it thickly with pitch. They put the Queen and her infant in the

barrel and rolled it down to the sea. Thus were the false orders from Tsar Saltan obeyed.

The stars shone brightly in the sky. The waves rolled peacefully over the ocean, and here and there a cloud misted the horizon. On and on floated the barrel. Inside it the poor Queen lay in tears. She strained and struggled to get out, while the baby boy went on growing.

As the Queen wept for their cruel fate, the boy implored the waves to drive them to land.

"Waves, O waves," he cried, "you are free to go where you will, on rocks or on beaches. O you who bear up mighty ships, do not destroy us but bring us safe to land."

The waves heard the child. Gently they drove the barrel ashore and silently ebbed back to the ocean.

Mother and child knew they were saved. Beneath the barrel they felt firm ground. But how were they to get out of it?

The boy stood upright and pressed his head against the top of the barrel.

"Let us make an opening," he said.

The top of the barrel broke, and the boy was able to climb out. He and his mother were free at last to wander where they would.

In the midst of a plain there was a hill. On it grew a single great oak. The boy said to himself that it was time to think about supper. He broke a branch from the tree. A cross on his breast hung from a silken cord. With the cord and the branch he fashioned a bow, and made an arrow of a smaller branch. Then with the bow and arrow he went down to the valley to look for game. No sooner had he reached the shore than he heard the sound of groaning. At the water's edge he saw a strange sight.

As he drew nearer he saw a white swan struggling in the shallow water. A hawk with outstretched talons and blood-stained beak hovered over her. At once the arrow sped from the boy's bow. It pierced the neck of the hawk, which with an unearthly cry dropped into the water. Round and round the hawk circled the swan, pecking at him with her beak and beating him with her wings, until the hawk vanished into the depths of the sea. Then the swan spoke to the boy in his own tongue.

"My prince," she said, "you have saved my life and set me free. You have lost your arrow, and perhaps you will have no food for three days. But be comforted. Misfortune is often a blessing in disguise. I will repay you well and do everything you bid me. It is not a swan but a maiden you have saved. It is not a hawk you have slain, but a dreaded magician. Go, and be of good heart. Get some sleep: that is best."

With these words the white swan flew off, leaving the Prince and his mother feeling hungry and distressed. Even though they had nothing to eat, they decided it would be best to get a good night's sleep.

As soon as the Prince awoke he rubbed his eyes in amazement. There before him stood a great city. Within its turreted walls and battlements rose the onion-shaped domes of churches and monasteries. At once he roused the Queen. Mother and son marvelled at what they saw and gave thanks for the swan's magnificent gift.

Together they went up to the city and entered its gates. They were welcomed by a great crowd, a pealing of bells and the sound of holy choirs raising their voices in thanks to God. Then came courtiers, riding in gold carriages, who welcomed the newcomers and greeted the Prince as their ruler. He was

named Prince Gvidon and received a cap of black fur, so that all should know he was ruler.

Gaily the wind swept over the waters, driving before it a ship with billowing sails. The mariners saw with astonishment that a new and wonderful city had sprung up on an island in their course. They

saw its onion-shaped domes of gold, its mighty walls, its sheltered harbour. As they approached they were saluted by guns, and Prince Gvidon signalled them to put in at the harbour. He gave them food and wine and asked them for tidings of the world.

"We have been selling furs of sable and silver fox," they told him. "Now we sail eastwards by way of the island of Buyan, whence we shall return to the kingdom of Tsar Saltan."

"Give the Tsar my greetings," said Prince Gvidon.

Then he bade the mariners farewell and lingered on the quay, watching them depart with tears in his eyes.

Just then the swan appeared on the waters and asked the Prince why he was sad.

"I would have liked to see my father," said Gvidon.

"That is easy," answered the swan. "I will turn you into a mosquito, and you can follow the ship."

She flapped her wings and splashed the sea water about her. Some of the scattered water fell upon Gvidon, who was instantly changed into a mosquito. He soon caught up with the ship and found himself a hiding-place in a crack in its timbers.

Gaily the wind swept over the water, driving before it the ship with billowing sails. Before long

the ship had passed the island of Buyan and was nearing the kingdom of Tsar Saltan. The Tsar sent orders that the mariners were to be welcomed home and visit him in his palace. As they went in the young Prince followed, still in the disguise of a mosquito. There he saw his father the Tsar sitting in the great hall upon a splendid throne. He wore shining armour and a crown of pure gold. But the eyes of the Tsar were sad and brooding.

On the steps of the throne stood the weaver, the cook and the old matchmaker, Babarikha. The Tsar asked the mariners what sights they had seen on their voyage. They told him of the beautiful

new city they had seen on an island where no city had been before. They ended their story by giving the Tsar the greetings of Prince Gvidon.

"If I live long enough", said Tsar Saltan, "I would like to visit that city and be the guest of its ruler."

But the weaver and the cook and old Babarikha put their heads together to see how they could stop him going.

"Good heavens!" said the cook with a sneer. "What a surprise to see a city on the seashore! But I can tell you about something still more marvellous. Somewhere there grows a tall fir tree, and under it sits a magic squirrel. This squirrel sings to herself as she cracks her nuts, and all the nuts have shells of pure gold and emerald kernels. Now that's what *I* call a miracle!"

Everyone began talking about the marvellous squirrel, but the young Prince felt himself growing angry. Buzzing loudly as he circled round the hall, he swooped down on his aunt the cook and stung her on her right eye. Everyone began chasing the mosquito, but he flew swiftly out of the open window and before long he was safe at home.

Once more Prince Gvidon walked by the shore, thinking sadly of his father and how he might reach him. Again the swan came up to him and asked how she might help. Gvidon told her about the miraculous squirrel, and said he didn't believe the story was true.

"Do not be sad," said the swan. "There really is such a squirrel, and I shall be only too happy to do what I can for you."

Cheered by his meeting with the swan, Gvidon went back to his palace in a happier mood. And what did he see there? Under a tall fir tree in the middle of the courtyard sat a little squirrel. She cracked the golden shells of her nuts, took out the emerald kernels and piled them up in neat little heaps. All the while she sang a song about gardens. Gvidon was delighted by what he saw and heard. He was loud in his praise of the swan, and gave orders that a crystal house should be built for the squirrel and men set to guard it. A clerk was appointed to keep a strict account of all the golden shells and the precious nuts.

Gaily the wind swept over the water, driving before it the ship with billowing sails. Onward sped the ship, towards the island, towards the city. Once more guns were fired. Orders were given that the mariners were to be welcomed on shore. Again Prince Gvidon gave them a banquet and asked how they had fared. The merchants replied that they had been round the world selling horses and ponies. They had been to the court of Tsar Saltan, and they were now on their way to see him again. Gvidon wished them god-speed, and once more sent his greetings to the Tsar.

Gvidon watched them go with tears in his eyes. Once more the swan came up to him.

"How I wish I could have gone with the mariners on their voyage," he said.

The swan circled round him, spraying him with water from head to foot. This time he was turned into a fly. At once he flew after the ship, caught her up and hid in a crack in the timbers.

Gaily the wind swept over the water, driving before it the ship with billowing sails, past the island of Buyan to the kingdom of Tsar Saltan. Once more the mariners were invited to the Tsar's court and given a banquet. He asked them about their travels. Prince Gvidon, disguised as a fly, followed them into the palace.

There sat Tsar Saltan in his gleaming armour and golden crown. On his face was the sad look that Gvidon had seen before. Around him stood the weaver and the cook and Babarikha. The mariners told their tale of the marvellous city by the sea.

"This time", they said, "we saw something even more wonderful. In the middle of the palace courtyard there is now a tall fir tree. Under it is a crystal house, in which lives a magic squirrel. The squirrel sits there, cracking nuts with golden shells and taking out kernels of pure emerald. All the time she sings songs. She has many servants and is saluted by her

guards. A special clerk has been appointed to keep a strict account of all the treasure. The shells are melted down to make gold coins, and the jewels are stored in the treasury. Everyone in the kingdom is rich. Everyone enjoys a life of luxury. Prince Gvidon once more sends you his greetings."

"If I live long enough", said the Tsar once again, "I should like to visit that city and be the guest of Prince Gvidon."

But the weaver and the cook and the old match-maker, Babarikha, were determined he should not go. With a sly wink the weaver said:

"What's so wonderful about a squirrel who cracks

golden nuts and piles up emeralds? Besides, we don't even know if the tale is true. I can tell you of another miracle. Somewhere there is a beach where the sea swells up with a deafening roar, then boils over. The beach is flooded, and when the waves divide there stand thirty-three fine-looking knights.

They are all the same height, and every one is a giant in shining armour. Behind them stands old Uncle Chernamor. Now that's what I call a wonderful sight!"

Tsar Saltan marvelled at this tale, but some of the guests took it with a pinch of salt. As for Gvidon, he was bursting with anger. He buzzed round and round the room and landed on the left eye of his aunt the weaver, which he bit as hard as he was able. In the noise and excitement that followed he flew out of the window and winged his way home.

Once again Gvidon walked alone beside the sea. Once again the swan came up to him. So the Prince told her of the latest marvel he had heard about.

"How much I should like", he said, "to have guardsmen like that in my kingdom."

"Have no care," replied the swan. "Why, those knights are my brothers, and you shall see them for yourself."

So the Prince climbed a tower in the palace and gazed towards the sea. On a deserted beach the

boiling waters rushed. Then they ebbed back, leaving three-and-thirty handsome knights marching in formation. Their leader was old Uncle Chernamor. Gvidon came down from the tower and welcomed them at the city gates.

"The swan has sent us," said old Uncle Chernamor. "From now on we will come out of the water every day and guard your kingdom."

So saying, he led his band back into the sea.

Gaily the wind swept over the water, driving before it the ship with billowing sails. When it reached the island guns were fired, and Gvidon invited the mariners to visit him. This time they told him they had been round the world selling gold, silver and steel. Now they were on their way back to the kingdom of Tsar Saltan, past the island of Buyan. Once again the Prince wished them god-speed and sent greetings to his father the Tsar.

Sadly Gvidon paced the shore, gazing out to sea. Up came the swan and asked what was the matter. He told her how he longed to follow the merchants. So she turned him into a bumble-bee, and he soon caught up with the ship.

Gaily the wind swept over the water, driving before it the ship with billowing sails, past the island of Buyan to the kingdom of Tsar Saltan. Guns were

fired in salute to welcome the merchants into the harbour. As they entered the Tsar's palace the bumble-bee followed them. In the throne-room sat his father in his shining armour and gold crown, but his eyes were sad and brooding. Around him stood the cook, the weaver and old Babarikha. With their four good eyes they watched the Tsar narrowly.

Once more the Tsar and his people talked with the mariners about the marvels of the voyage. This time the visitors told of the three-and-thirty tall knights from the sea who now marched around Gvidon's island and made it the best defended kingdom in Christendom. Then the merchants gave the Tsar greetings from Gvidon.

"If I live long enough", said the Tsar, "I shall pay a visit to the kingdom of Gvidon."

The weaver and the cook dared not say a word. But Babarikha, the old matchmaker, smirked and said:

"What's so marvellous about people marching out of the sea? And how do we know the story's true? What *I* have heard is that somewhere there dwells a princess so beautiful that none can take his eyes from her. She is more glorious than the sun in the sky, and at night she lights up the earth. In her hair the moonbeams play. On her forehead shines a star. She has the stately walk of a peacock and her

voice is the voice of a stream that sings. Now that's what *I* call a sight worth seeing."

The courtiers wisely said nothing, but the Tsar was interested. As for Gvidon, in a towering rage he buzzed and buzzed round the hall until he landed on Babarikha's nose and stung it with all his might.

By the time the commotion had died down the bee had flown from the open window and was soon safe at home.

Sadly the Prince walked by the seashore, and the swan came up and asked what was the matter.

"I am sad," he said, "I am lonely. I need a companion to share my life. But I have heard of a wonderful princess with moonbeams in her hair and a star on her forehead. From now on none but this princess can please me. Only she can be my bride. I am ready to go to the world's end to find her."

"I know that princess," answered the swan. "But think well before you start such a journey."

Then, when Gvidon said that no power on earth would make him change his mind, she confessed that she herself was the princess. Up into the air she flew and came down some distance away. Then she shook herself and turned into a princess. In her hair the moonbeams played. On her forehead shone a star. She spoke like a singing stream and walked as if on air. When she drew close to him, Gvidon folded her in his arms. Together they went and knelt before Gvidon's mother, the Queen, and asked her blessing. Soon they were married and living happily together. With great joy they waited for the coming of their first child.

Gaily the wind swept over the water, driving before it the ship with billowing sails towards Gvidon's kingdom. Guns were fired in salute. The merchants were welcomed to the palace. A banquet was given in their honour.

"What have you been carrying," asked Gvidon, "and whither are you bound?"

When Gvidon learned that they had been carrying contraband, and were now on their way to the kingdom of Tsar Saltan, he said:

"Bear my greetings to the Tsar and tell him I still await his coming."

But this time the Prince did not follow the ship. He could not bear to leave his wife.

Gaily the wind swept over the water, driving before it the ship with billowing sails, past the island of Buyan to the kingdom of Tsar Saltan. Again the mariners were invited to the palace. Again they spoke of the wonders of the voyage—the miraculous squirrel with her gold and emerald nuts, the three and thirty tall knights with their leader, Uncle Chernamor, guardians of the island, and the surpassing beauty of the Princess. This was more than the Tsar could bear. He at once resolved to visit the island. In vain did the cook, the weaver and Babarikha, the old matchmaker, implore him not to go.

"Let my ships be made ready!" he commanded.

At his window in the tower stood Prince Gvidon. He gazed far out to sea. Towards the horizon he made out a number of specks. He took up his spy-glass and saw that the specks were Tsar Saltan's fleet. On the deck of the flagship stood the Tsar himself. Amongst the people round him were the cook, the weaver and old Babarikha. They gazed with astonishment at the wonderful island as it rose before them.

Swiftly the Prince ran down the steps and welcomed the visitors at the city gates. There stood the three and thirty knights, drawn up as a guard of honour. As they entered the courtyard, the Tsar beheld the miraculous squirrel in its crystal dwelling under the fir tree. Then he was greeted by the most

beautiful princess he had ever set eyes on. In her hair the moonbeams played. On her forehead gleamed a star.

Beside the Princess stood Gvidon's mother, the Queen. Overjoyed, the Tsar recognized his long-lost wife. In terror the cook, the weaver and old Babarikha ran and hid themselves. But they were found and driven out of hiding. Then they confessed their wrongdoings and begged to be forgiven. So the Tsar, delighted to be with his family once more, merely sent them back home. Then a great banquet was held in celebration, and everyone feasted, drank and was happy.